The Elves and the Storymaker

For Nelly and Isla Wade,
with Seriously Silly Wishes
L.A.

For Sophia and Olivia
A.R.

Visit Laurence Anholt's website at
www.anholt.co.uk

ORCHARD BOOKS
338 Euston Road
London NW3 3BH
Orchard Books Australia
Level 17-207 Kent Street, Sydney, NSW 2000, Australia

First published by Orchard Books in 2008
First paperback publication in 2009

Text © Laurence Anholt 2008
Illustrations © Arthur Robins 2008

The rights of Laurence Anholt to be identified as the author
and of Arthur Robins to be identified as the illustrator
of this work have been asserted by them in accordance
with the Copyright, Designs and Patents Act, 1988.

A CIP catalogue record for this book is available from the British Library.

ISBN 978 1 84616 074 5 (hardback)
ISBN 978 1 84616 312 8 (paperback)

1 2 3 4 5 6 7 8 9 10 (hardback)
1 2 3 4 5 6 7 8 9 10 (paperback)

Printed in China

Orchard Books is a division of Hachette Children's Books,
an Hachette Livre UK company.
www.hachettelivre.co.uk

Laurence Anholt   Arthur Robins

seriously SILLY colour

The Elves and the Storymaker

ORCHARD BOOKS

There was once a silly Storymaker and his wife who were very poor.

The old man hadn't sold a story in years and they had nothing to eat but old story books with cheese on top.

One evening, sitting in front
of his dusty old computer,
the Storymaker realised that
he couldn't start a new story
because he didn't have a single
idea in his head.

"Well, that's it!" he told his wife.
"I will never write another book."
"Don't worry," she said. "Leave
your computer and come to bed."

As the silly Storymaker had no
ideas, he had no dreams at all
and he slept deeply until morning.

When he went down in the
morning, he was amazed to
see that there was the beginning
of a story printed neatly next
to his computer.

He sat down and read it carefully
- it was a brilliant beginning!
"Whoever can have written this?"
he asked his wife.

"Well, husband," she replied,
"in the night I heard a tiny noise:

tippety

tap,

tippety

tap!

I crept downstairs and saw two teeny elves beginning your story. They were singing as they worked:

"Elves!" laughed the Story maker,
"You're making up stories!"
"It's true," said his wife,
"and there's the beginning of
the story to prove it."

"If only I could think of a *middle*
bit for the story," he told his wife.
"A scary bit would be good."

That night, he went to bed as before. And when he came down in the morning, there was the middle bit of the story waiting for him. It was better than ever and really scary.

"Whoever can have written this?" he asked his wife again.

"Well, husband," she replied,
"in the night I heard a scary noise:

tippety

tap,

tippety

tap!

I felt very frightened,
but I crept downstairs.
Suddenly, I saw two huge
gorillas writing your story.
They were singing
as they worked:

"Gorillas!" laughed the Storymaker,
"You're making up stories!"
"It's true," said his wife, "and
there's the middle of the story
to prove it."

"If only I could think of some silly jokes," he told his wife, "the story would be even better still."

That night he went to bed as before. And when he came down in the morning, there was the story with lots of silly jokes.

"Whoever can have written these silly jokes?" he giggled.

"Well, husband," she replied,
"in the night I heard a noise:

zippety
zap,
zippety
zap!

I crept downstairs and saw two silly aliens writing jokes. They were singing as they worked:

"Aliens!" laughed the Storymaker,
"You must be joking!"
"It's true," said his wife, "and
there's the silly story to prove it."

"All we need now is an end
for the story," said the author,
"but I haven't got any ideas at all."

That evening, the old story writer
went to bed as before. But in the
middle of the night, he woke up.
He heard a funny noise:

> tippety tap,
>> tippety tap!

"I will go and thank the person
who has written this fantastic
story," he said.

He crept out of bed and down the stairs. Someone was singing in the kitchen:

...his wife!

"You *have* been making up stories!" he said.

"Yes," she said. "And now we can sell the story and buy all the food we need. And a brand new computer."

The old man gave his wife
a big kiss. Then they sat
down at the table side by side
and read the story.

It had a brilliant beginning.
It had a scary middle.
It had lots of silly jokes.
But the best bit of all was . . .

THE

END!

ENJOY ALL THESE SERIOUSLY SILLY STORIES!

Bleeping Beauty	ISBN 978 1 84616 073 8
The Elves and the Storymaker	ISBN 978 1 84616 074 5
The Silly Willy Billy Goats	ISBN 978 1 84616 075 2
The Ugly Duck Thing	ISBN 978 1 84616 076 9
Freddy Frog Face	ISBN 978 1 84616 077 6
Handsome and Gruesome	ISBN 978 1 84616 078 3
The Little Marzipan Man	ISBN 978 1 84616 079 0
The Princess and the Tree	ISBN 978 1 84616 080 6

All priced at £8.99

Orchard books are available from all good bookshops, or can be ordered direct from the publisher:
Orchard Books, PO BOX 29, Douglas IM99 1BQ
Credit card orders please telephone: 01624 836000 or fax: 01624 837033
or visit our website: www.orchardbooks.co.uk or e-mail: bookshop@enterprise.net for details.

To order please quote title, author and ISBN and your full name and address.
Cheques and postal orders should be made payable to 'Bookpost plc.'
Postage and packing is FREE within the UK (overseas customers should add £1.00 per book).

Prices and availability are subject to change.